ד.

The Diary of an Old Drunk

George

The
Diary
of an
Old
Drunk

George Bothamley

Matador
9 Priory Business Park,
Wistow Road, Kibworth Beauchamp,
Leicestershire. LE8 0RX
Tel: 0116 279 2299
Email: books@troubador.co.uk
Web: www.troubador.co.uk/matador
Twitter: @matadorbooks

ISBN 978 1788036 542

British Library Cataloguing in Publication Data.
A catalogue record for this book is available from the British Library.

Printed and bound by CPI Group (UK) Ltd, Croydon, CR0 4YY
Typeset in 11pt Minion Pro by Troubador Publishing Ltd, Leicester, UK

Matador is an imprint of Troubador Publishing Ltd

For Grace

Introduction

It was sheer, blind chance that I happened upon the writings which make up what I have come to call The Diary of an Old Drunk. And in truth, it is not strictly a diary; more a collection of various thoughts, experiences and poetry – some connected, others more singular. In that sense, I suppose it is part diary, part philosophical work, part poetry anthology and part autobiography.

I came across it one day when I was caught in a heavy rain shower while walking unfamiliar streets. I had taken cover in an old bus shelter, and, as I sat waiting for the rain to pass (or at least to ease somewhat so I could resume my long walk home), I noticed, just by my foot, a small, beaten up book, bound in a dirty brown leather cover.

Had it been anything else on the floor that day, I am sure I would have simply ignored it. But, for some reason, I felt an overwhelming sense of curiosity towards the little book. I simply had to know what, if anything, was inside it.

So, as the rain continued to pour outside of the shelter, I gently reached down.

And what I discovered far exceeded anything I could have imagined.

On the very first page, there was a block of scribbled writing… which I soon realized was a poem. Untitled, and unsigned – it was quite unlike any poem I had read before, but, frankly, one of the most powerful things I had ever read.

Then, as I flicked through the rest of the pages, I found that they too were all filled, from top to bottom, with words by this same scruffy hand.

The spelling was, at times, a little shaky; the grammar was not always accurate; the thoughts were not always consistent, and the language was often far from delicate. But even so, I was completely absorbed by it all. It was raw, intense, emotional, and, more than anything, brutally honest.

I remember remaining in that bus shelter, reading entry after entry, long after the rain had ceased, and well into the early evening – at which point the light around me began to fade, and I finally decided to head home. Of course, I did not hesitate in taking the book with me – and over the next few weeks, I read and re-read the diary over and over again… until I knew the majority of it off by heart.

I was so captivated by it all that I even took to carrying it with me wherever I went – as if it were my own personal diary. A habit which, as you can imagine, did not escape the attention of the people closest to me.

I am told that each of them had their own unique theory

about what could possibly be so special about this tatty book of mine– until finally, when we were all gathered one evening for dinner in a local restaurant, the question was addressed to me directly.

Just what was in this book?

Having been put on the spot so dramatically, and with the whole table now leaning in, I initially found it a little hard to explain my discovery.

But, as I went on, I drew the book out of my pocket, and I must have become quite animated, because, before I knew it, I had most of the restaurant listening to me as I read my favourite entries out loud.

By the time I finished that night, everybody around me – friends, waiters and strangers – all wanted to read the rest of the diary for themselves.

But, of course, they could not all borrow the book at the same time (and, even if they could, I was still rather reluctant to part with the actual thing at this point)

So, I promised an alternative. I would type up a word for word copy, which could then be printed off as many times as necessary, and distributed freely to anyone who wanted to read it.

And so it was that this transcription of The Diary of an Old Drunk was born.

But, seeing as, in this case, I am merely the copyist, I would like to take a moment to briefly write a few words about the real author of the Diary.

Over the course of time, I have made numerous attempts to try and discover more about the man I have come to know as The Old Drunk.

I conducted extensive enquiries in and around the area of the bus shelter where I found the diary; asking in all of the local cafés, bars, hotels, shops and nightclubs.

I also spoke with many of the local bus drivers, taxi drivers, postmen, traffic wardens and police officers – anyone I could think of that had a day to day connection with the streets.

And, on top of this (in a case of life beginning to imitate art), I even started frequenting many of the well-known homeless "hot spots" within close proximity to the bus shelter – in the hope of at least picking up on The Old Drunk's trail.

But, though I gained many new friends during my investigations (and heard many more truly remarkable life stories), I did not manage to gain another morsel of information regarding The Old Drunk.

I spoke to tramps, prostitutes, graffiti artists, drug dealers, market stall owners, magazine sellers, street cleaners and dog walkers – and not a single one of them could tell me anything about him. And, perhaps even more damning to my investigations, not a single person even recognised any of the places he mentions in his writings.

I was therefore forced to conclude that the area in which I found the diary was, in all likelihood, not the area in which the diary was written. And, in that case, there were (and are) quite literally thousands of other towns or cities where this diary could potentially have been written ... which leaves little hope for ever pinning the man down.

And herein lies the biggest problem with the diary – and with The Old Drunk himself.

Because, while he uses this diary to record his innermost thoughts, feelings and experiences – he is almost completely silent when it comes to actual details about himself.

We can confidently gather that he is a man in the later stages of life; but he never gives us his age or any solid physical descriptions. He also never gives any details about his family, or his childhood. He never even mentions his own name.

And regarding the area in which he lives at the time of writing, at best, he may mention the nickname of a non-specific area – but otherwise, we are just given vague references to fairly generic landmarks: a hotel, a shop, etc. which, as I have already said, could apply to a thousand and one places.

So with no clues as to who the man was, or where he was from, the only other hope I had was to track down the people who may have known him (or known of him).
But again, this led me to another disappointing dead end.

While he does mention one or two names over the course of the diary, once again, they are often only nicknames. And even when they are seemingly genuine, he only ever gives first names. Never surnames.
So even his acquaintances are shrouded in mystery.

In the end, I was forced to resign myself to the fact that the man who wrote this diary is destined to remain forever nameless. (That is, unless there are any detectives out there…?)

But, aside from the questions concerning who The Old Drunk is or where he was from, there are also two other questions which I have regularly been asked since first distributing this diary.

They are:

Do you still have the diary?

And

Can I see it?

Unfortunately, the answer to both of those questions is No.

Since the very moment I picked the diary up from the floor of the bus shelter – and certainly throughout my time transcribing it – I had been really quite torn as to what I should do with the it.

A large part of me wanted nothing else than to keep it for myself … to treasure it.

But, at the same time, I always had this underlying feeling in me that this book was not intended to be kept safe in a house, or on a bookshelf, or inside a drawer. In short, it was not meant to be treasured by someone like me.

Its rightful place was, and is, on the streets.

And so, once I had finished copying out the final entry, I returned to that old bus shelter.

I placed the book back down on the very spot where I had found it, and I walked away – knowing that, from there, it can continue on the journey which it has been on since slipping from the hands of its creator, The Old Drunk.

Who knows where it could end up next!

But, even though I no longer have the actual book, the words, the stories, and the man, will stay with me for ever. In the very first entry of his diary, The Old Drunk says "… it's my hope that if I write them, then my words will survive // Inside // The minds of others // Maybe they'll sympathize …"

And I only hope that I can help him to succeed in this.

George Samuel Bothamley

Entry 1

I write these words in preparation for the day that I die
'Cause I won't get no horse drawn carriage
And ain't no-one gonna cry
How can they shed a tear for someone
They didn't know was alive?
But it's my hope that if I write them then my words will survive
Inside
The minds of others
Maybe they'll sympathize
If I talk about what it's like to see the world through my eyes
See I've
Lived such a long time, lived a life full of lies
Spending my days stuck in a bottle, as the world passed me by.

Imagine
What it feels like when your mind's a violent peace
When you're bursting full of black thoughts you can't ever release
When it's

1

Faith that you seek
But you got no belief
And you're too weak to even speak.

Can you picture a world where you're feeling like this?
Where your heart's an abyss
Where you barely exist
And you scream when you sleep, seeing faces in the mist
Places you miss
And the girls you coulda kissed
But you're fifty-seven years too late.

And every second you're awake, haunted by your mistakes
Nothing left to lose
How much more of this could you take?
As the ground starts to shake
And your heart starts to break
Fell in love and got covered in hate.

Well, if there's one thing I learnt
From all the things I been through
The stars don't shine on the lonely
Child, they're laughing at you

You shouldn't try to be someone
'Cause you're nobody new

When all you wanted was the world
But the world didn't want you.

Entry 2

You know – folks round here call me all kinds of things.
They call me a waster, a good for nothing, a drunk.
All sorts.
And I don't mind, really.
Hell, I know I ain't no prince charming.
And they're right, I *am* good for nothing.
I *am* a useless drunk.

But sometimes I hear people calling me a tramp
And man, this gets on my last nerve.

See, here's what people don't understand.
Guys like me, we come in three types:
Hobos,
Tramps,
And Bums.

A Hobo is a fella who's got no home,
But wants to work
And *will* travel.

A Tramp is a fella who's got no home

And wants to work,
But *won't* travel.

And a Bum is a fella who's got no home
Doesn't want to work
And won't travel.

Now see, I been in this line of work most of my life.
And one thing I can tell you is that being on the streets
really ain't no different to working in an office.
You know, you start by making the teas
And you end up having the teas made for you.

So, I started as Hobo.
I became a Tramp
And finished up as a Bum.

And here's the thing.
You wouldn't go round calling some chief executive a tea
maker, would you?
A tea maker wants to be called a tea maker
And a boss wants to be called a boss.

So, when I was a tramp, I didn't want to be called a bum.
And now I'm a bum
I ain't nobody's tramp.

Entry 3

You know, something hit me not too long ago:
I am literally the only person I know.

That's kind of strange, right?

They say everybody is somebody,
And everybody has somebody else.
Well, not me.
I'm no-one
And I got no-one else.

But being no-one
And having no-one –
It's kinda funny.
'Cause actually, if I'm no-one
Then, in a sense, I'm *everyone* as well.

So now, when some girly in town calls me a drunk, I say to her
"Hey, I'm the most sober guy I know!"

Or if a kid calls me old, I can say
"Maybe ... but I'm the youngest guy I know!"

'Cause that's exactly the truth.
It ain't no lie.

Look at it,
If I'm the only guy I know
Then I'm the ugliest guy I know
And the best looking guy I know too.

If I'm the only guy I know
Then as far as I'm concerned
I'm the most intelligent,
And the dumbest,
The richest,
And the poorest,
The hardest,
The softest,
The deepest,
And the shallowest guy I know.

I'm the kindest,
The most selfish,
The tallest,
The smallest,
The wisest,
And the most foolish guy I know.

I'm the highest,
The lowest,

The fastest,
The slowest,
The warmest,
The softest,
The loudest,
The most silent,
The meekest,
And the most violent,
The funniest,
And the least funny guy I know.

Now, ain't that something?

When you look at it like that,
Well … I guess you could say I've got the best life,
And the worst.

And you know, when I *do* look at it like that
I don't know whether to laugh …
Or cry.

Entry 4

I got myself £16.49 yesterday.
So I decided to treat myself to a dinner in the swanky hotel in town.

Well, I couldn't afford no dinner.
But I know for a fact they do sandwiches there in the afternoon for like twelve pound something.
So I fancied getting me one of them.

Here's what happened.

I walked right into the place, and sat down in the bar area.
I guess I was getting all kinds of looks; I didn't really pay attention to be honest.
I just sat down, and waited ...
Well, shit, they call that place high class,
But I had to wait near on ten minutes for someone to come over and offer to serve me.

And when they did, it was the manager – accompanied by some spotty face kid.

I thought "*Imagine that,*
Little old me, with £16.49 in my pocket, getting this VIP
treatment,
Having the manager himself coming to serve me."
I was honoured.

So, I looked up at him and his spotty sidekick
And he said "May I help you?"

I said "Yeah, you can help … can I get me one of these
steak sandwiches?"

The manager guy looked around a little,
Like he was hoping to find some way to fob me off.
In the end, he just said
"I'm sorry … we don't … we don't serve guys like you."

Now, that's cold.
That's a cold thing for someone to say to you:
"*We don't serve guys like you.*"

So, I looked at him
And said
"Well, I don't eat guys like me either.
Just get me a goddamn steak sandwich."

He didn't move.
Just stood there and said "I'm going to have to ask you to leave."

With that, I reached into my pocket – taking out every
penny of the £16.49.

And, I admit – I slammed this money down so hard on the table that I damn nearly broke it ... but come on, I was hungry.

A guy does crazy things when he's got a craving for a sandwich.

Then, I started shouting, so everyone in the place could hear

"Look, I got money, that's what you want ain't it? Money. Well, look. Ain't nothing worse about my money than anyone else's. So give me a goddamn steak sandwich."

With that, the manager called out for security, and before I knew it these two big ass guys were on me like a disease. I tried to grab for my money, but instead caught the table cloth and pulled it clean off.

Man, that caused one hell of a noise.

The table rocked, all the cutlery hit the floor, and I think a couple of the wine glasses smashed too.

It was chaos.

Anyway, before I knew it I was being thrown out the door.

Actually, that's a lie.

Apparently I wasn't even good enough to be thrown onto their shiny ass doorstep, so these two security guys escorted me like 50 yards away, to throw me down on some other sucker's doorstep.

The whole time, I kept asking for my £16.49,
But they just told me to shut the fuck up.

And you know, I never did get my money back.

Can you believe that?

You'd think a high class place like that would be above robbing an old man of his £16.49.

Well I won't be dining there again, that's for sure.

Give me a bin with a half-eaten packet of crisps any day.

Entry 5

In every place I ever been, there's always a hierarchy.

Some guys compare the streets to the jungle, but they're wrong.

The truth is, the streets are more like the school playground.

The guys out here aren't animals – they're just kids.

You've got the young hustlers – they're like the school football team –

Then the prostitutes are like the cheerleaders, or the popular girls.

The drug dealers are like the school bullies – walking around with their skinny ass young henchmen.

And then you occasionally get the odd ambitious guy come along trying to muscle in on the turf of either the drug dealers or the hustlers. He's like the new kid in school, whose parents are always moving house … he usually won't last long.

And as for me?

Well, I got told once that I was a teacher – but I think that's bullshit.

I'm more like the caretaker.

I'm that weird janitor, who has worked at the school forever, but never does a thing except sit in his little cupboard all day, talking to his broomsticks.

Entry 6

It's true that there's a lot of competition out here.
A lot of people wanting to rule the streets.
But I don't bother with all that shit.
Never have – never will.

Don't get me wrong, I'm not scared.
I never been scared of a single person in my life – not drug
dealers, hustlers, pimps … nobody.
But I just never been interested in ruling the streets.
I'm too old now anyway, but even when I was young –
It's just too much hassle.
Too much work.

I'm serious.
I mean, if you want to rule the streets it's a full time
profession.
You've got to buy gear,
Sell gear,
Talk with people,
Go places,
Keep up your rep –
Even fight every now and then.

No, no, no, no, no.

Leave that to all the other suckers – I'm happy just to do my own thing,

Keep myself to myself.

Besides, I know every drug dealer round here now, and they know me.

So I do get a certain amount of protection these days anyway.

It's funny.

I remember when I first came round here – I used to always be getting offered drugs.

Seriously, every single day I'd get offered some shit.

And every other day I'd get threatened too.

With some clown or another trying to intimidate me or getting up in my face.

Man, I used to get beaten up twice a month and robbed once a week.

But now –

They all know me.

They know I'm no trouble.

They know drink is my poison, not drugs – and they know there ain't nobody that can get a drink cheaper than I can.

So we get on alright.

And as for the prostitutes?

Well, they do occasionally come up to me, usually either 'cause one of the other girlys has dared them to – or, failing that, only if they're having a real slow night … at the end of a real slow week … in a real slow month.

But any time they do, I have the same answer for them. "Child, I'm too old for hookers now."

Entry 7

I guess I should describe this old town a little.

Although, there really ain't too much to describe.

It's all just betting shops,
Bus stops,
Rain drops
And bottle tops.

Oh, and every now and then,
You hear the sound of gun shots.

Entry 8

I wonder if there's a heaven for Bums.

You know, most people are afraid to die;
I guess 'cause they've got too much life to be living.
And besides, most people don't know what, if anything, is
waiting for them on the other side.

But me?
Nah, I'm not afraid to die.
I can't afford to be.

The way I see it, most people can run away from the shit
they fear; or ignore the big questions.
They can hide behind their job, or their car, or their house.
They can distract themselves with raising a couple kids, or
with getting married and shit like that.
But guys like me, we ain't got that luxury.
We got no place to hide.

I compare it to facing the weather.
When it's cold, most people can hide from it by putting on
another layer of clothes, or by keeping warm in their homes.

Same when it's raining – most people can hide under an umbrella and such.

But guys like me, we have to acclimatise to it all.

We don't want to.

Man, I'd much rather be indoors watching some shit on the TV on those cold winter nights.

But, like I said, we have to.

Guys like me, we have to face this weather.

'Cause we've got nowhere else to go

And it's the same with our thoughts.

Now, I may have been a good for nothing all my life.

But I'm not afraid of what happens when we die.

Boy, I'd be just as happy being a meal for a worm as I would be living on a cloud.

But Heaven ain't some place on a cloud anyway.

In my mind, Heaven is a bar.

And life is just stepping outside for a moment to have a cigarette.

So here we are, standing outside, with our family and a bunch of our friends.

And we're all smoking together, and talking, and having a good time.

And maybe while we're all out here, a couple of strangers come along and ask for a light, and we get talking to them as well.

Then, one by one, each person finishes their cigarette and heads back into the bar.

You might be the first of your friends to finish –
Or you might be the last,
But either way, when your cigarette has burnt out – you head on back into the bar.
And when you get in there – man, it's all happening.
There's music, and good food – and you get to hook up again with all the friends and family members who finished their cigarettes before you.

Just picture it.
A bunch of them will have already scored you a table by the fire, and bought a round of drinks.
Across the room, maybe a couple of them are shooting some pool, or throwing darts, or tearing up the fruit machines.
Or maybe a few of them are at the bar, mixing it with a few pretty girls.
It's all good.

So you sit down, take a sip of your cold beer and you just carry on having a good time.
While every so often, another friend finishes a cigarette and joins you all.

Entry 9

You know what?
Just like I say Heaven is a bar – and life is like smoking a cigarette
I know something else too.
This world is a casino.
This world is a casino – and we're all gamblers;
That's a cold fact.

Of course, some gamblers are always gonna be luckier than others.
You get some who can stay in the game for a long time,
Winning here and there.
While others straight up lose at their first hand.
You even get some who quit midway through the game,
'cause the stakes get too high and they can't handle it.
But at the end of it all – everybody winds up losing.
The house always wins, right?

The house always wins.

And see, what happens in this world is this:
The house throws you all kind of good odds at the start of the game.

It entices you to keep gambling.

It promises you that, if you only keep going a little longer, *you* can win big.

You can be the one to get the big prizes – Love, Wealth, Fame, Happiness … whatever else.

And most people fall for it.

They think "*This house ain't so bad … it's giving me a chance … damn, look at all these things I can win, I want to get me some of that … let me go ahead and take a couple chances here.*"

And so they take a bet

And another

And another.

Not realising that, all the while, the cards are stacked,

The dealer is crooked

And at the table alongside them is a bunch of hustlers, who are going to take them for everything they have.

That's exactly the truth of life – you're battling the odds constantly.

And half the time, you don't even know it.

You just think "*Damn, another loss … well, let me try again. I can feel a win coming.*"

Well let me tell you something.

There ain't a single person who's ever beaten this house.

Some people think they can.

Some people bet big a couple times

And win big
And it all looks fantastic.
They've won a stack of money.
Taken all the big prizes.
Everyone in the casino is in awe of them.

But it don't matter how much they take from the house,
At the end of it all, the house wins it back.

Sometimes, it physically takes all their winnings back …
pound for pound.
But a lot of times it doesn't.
A lot of times, it allows them to keep what they've won
'Cause while they have all their fame and wealth
The house takes even more from them.
It takes their innocence.
It takes their youth and their health.
It takes their love and their hope.
And eventually, it takes their life.

There ain't nobody who can escape those odds.

Entry 10

The streets are just dull.
That's exactly it.
People think living on the streets is hard 'cause of the cold
or the hunger or shit like that.
Boy, those things are nothing.
It's the boredom.
There just ain't nothing to do on the streets;
Not a damn thing.

There was a time when I used to people watch a lot – that
was my hobby.
But man, I seen every type of person three or four times
now, so there ain't no surprises for me there.

And other than that, what is there?
I can't afford to buy shit.
I got no person to visit, and no person to visit me.
I got no place I want to see – and sure as hell no place that
wants to see me.

I remember another thing I used to do a lot was think.
I would spend whole days, whole weeks, just thinking.

Thinking about life
Thinking about death
Thinking about everything else in between
(And a few things either side of them too.)

But man, my brain don't work like it used to.

Thinking is a young man's game I guess.

Entry 11

You know, I heard a saying once
"Every great journey, begins with a single step."

Well, yeah … but so do all the shitty journeys as well.

Every time you started out, got nowhere, and ended up back home…
Every time you tripped over and bruised your face or broke a bone…
Every time you got to where you wanted, and it ended up being a fucking hole…
All of those journeys started with a single step too you know.

That's why I say: Child, stay on the ground.
It's safer down here, and there's no chance of you falling down – 'cause you're already there.
Seriously, just sit back.
Relax.
And let everyone else do all the walking.

That's my advice.

Entry 12

No, I never was a worker.
Even when I worked, I never was a worker.

I had my one and only job when I was 19 years old – on a building site.
I used to make the tea.
Actually, that's a lie.
I was the "beverage maker's assistant".
So basically, washing cups for the guy who made the tea.
That was the level which best suited my talents.

I probably should have tried to progress,
But, honestly, I was never too desperate to leave my position as tea maker's cup washer.
Why would I?
I didn't like lifting tea mugs – so why the hell would I want to lift heavier shit like bricks and such?
That seemed like a step down if anything.

I remember one time, a guy actually offered me a chance to learn bricklaying.
Of course, I said no.

I said "Why would I want to learn something which forces me to work my ass off building a house for some clown, only so that, when it's built, and he's living in it with a wife and his kids, I won't ever be allowed to enter it? And, if I ever did step inside it, he'd either plain kick me out, or he'd kick the shit outta me..."

I said "Sorry, but that seems kinda pointless."

That really didn't go down well with the guy, but I didn't care – and I still don't.

I thought the same then as I do now – working is ridiculous.

I'll say it again – working is ridiculous.

It's even more stupid than slavery.

At least slaves are forced to work.

Most people actually *choose* to work.

And what for?

To pay for some house?

Right, they pay for that house which they never get to spend any time in – because they're always working.

Or how about to pay for a car?

Yeah, you know, that car they need mostly to be able to drive to and from work.

Oh, and some people work to pay for a holiday.

That's right, they work their ass off, and save up all year for a holiday that they only need because they've been working so damn hard.

Now that is insanity.

Entry 13

They say it's dangerous living on the streets.
And it can be.
For new guys, especially.

When you're new to this shit, you tend to overestimate
your own importance.
You go about thinking "OK, sure, guys get robbed out
here. Guys die out here. But it won't happen to me."
Man, let me tell you – it will happen.
And unless you understand that, and try to put some shit
in place to deal with it, it will happen again too.
And again.

See, me – I'm experienced now.
I don't get hassled much these days 'cause guys know
where I stand.
(Well … where I sit.)
But I've been through it all in my time.
Trust me.

I remember the worst time I ever got attacked.
It was ten … maybe fifteen years ago now.

For no reason, five young thugs, and two girlys, literally kicked the shit outta me.

To be honest, I remember knowing those punks were trouble as soon as I saw them.
They were shuffling on down the street together;
All pissed
And clearly looking for trouble.

But, understand this:
I see a group of assholes just like this at least three times a week.
And usually, they'll shout a few cuss words at you,
Maybe throw some shit or another
And then move along.
That's fine – it comes with the territory.
But, oh no.
This time, one of the girlys pointed in my direction and the seven of them came on over to get up in my face.

At first they were just cussing,
Saying I stank and shit like that.
Then one of the guys reached out at me and damn stole my hat from my head.
I mean, come on now – stealing from a homeless guy?
I remember thinking *"Is this really the way things work these days?"*
There's a whole high street full of jewellery shops and clothes shops within a hundred yard radius of where I was sat.
There's a whole neighbourhood full of houses and cars no more than a mile away.

And, if that's not enough, just outside of that, there's a whole fucking world of expensive shit to steal, if you're that way inclined.

But no – of all the things these guys could have stolen, they chose to steal a hat from a bum.

That tells you all you need to know I think.

Anyway, back to it.

So the guy took my hat – started throwing it around with his sniggering friends.

I didn't get up – I just politely asked them to give it back.

They didn't.

Then, admittedly by accident, one of the girlys kicked over my can of beer.

And with that, I got a little crazy.

Damn right I should too.

That can of drink was valuable to me.

I'd been rationing all day, to get me through the night

And there I was, watching it pour clean empty while they all just laughed.

So, I stood up.

I wasn't gonna do anything – I just thought I'd tell her off and, with any luck, make her replace it.

But see, I never was all that quick.

So I was actually only half up off my ass, when two of the guys put me straight back down on it again.

And together, they laid into me like I was a wrinkled old piñata.

But you know what, that wasn't even the worst part.
What was worse, was when one of the girls started chipping in.
Man, she was vicious as hell – and her high heel shoes where like fucking daggers.
I just lay there with my hands over my head, trying to shield myself as best as I could, and figuring "*Well, I guess I'm gonna die.*"

In the end, they gave me a few more kicks in the back, (and one of them – probably the girl – spat on me), then the seven of them ran off laughing – leaving me in a pile.

I remember I just lay there in a heap for a while, trying to figure out what the fuck had just happened.

I don't know how long I was there but, eventually, a couple of street preachers came along and helped me out.
They nursed me a little and called an ambulance.
They offered to call the police too, but I said no.
I'm a lot of things – but I'm not a grass.
And besides, I couldn't be bothered to go through all the hassle of going down to the station and explaining everything fifty times over.
So I just spun them some tale of how I'd taken a fall, and they left me alone.

It was only the next day that I realised I'd made a mistake.

If I'd only involved the police, then maybe they could have found my hat.

I never did get it back.

To this day, I try every now and then to get people on the case to search for it.

But mostly they just laugh at me and tell me to piss off.

How messed up is that?

If those punks had stolen some rich clown's car or his snooty ass wife's purse – all hell would break loose.

But an old guy gets his hat stolen, and nobody cares.

I paid good money for that hat too.

Had it for near on half my life.

Entry 14

I hear people grumbling all the time on the streets – mostly over nothing.

And I tell you – it gets on my last nerve.

You know, there are guys I've met – lived on the streets for five, ten, fifteen years … and they're still complaining.

They're saying "Man, I hate those police always waking me up – moving me on … all I'm tryin'a do is sleep, and they're shining a torch light in my eyes."

Or they're saying "Man, this weather … this cold … this heat … this rain … this drought …"

Honestly, they're never happy.

But what do they expect?

We're living on the streets, people – this ain't no hotel.

This ain't no holiday spa.

So sure, you're gonna get police on your case.

You're gonna get more bad days of weather than good days.

But all that crying and complaining don't do no good.

It don't change the weather.

It don't change nothing.

Entry 15

I wrote this little thing today.
It's called A Poem about Nothing.
And that's exactly what it's about –
Nothing.

Nothing to lose,
Nothing to win,
Nothing but blood and bones
Wrapped in dirty old skin;
And nothing ever goes wrong
If you don't try at all;
And nothing's waiting to catch you
Any time you fall.

They say everything has a price;
Well, nothing's given for free.
Nothing came of the things
That I hoped I would be.
And nothing makes me smile,
Nothing makes me cry,
Got nothing to live for
And no reason to die.

Our facts are nothing more
Than belief in disguise,
There's no such thing as the truth
Just more accurate lies.
And nothing's where I call home,
There isn't much here to do,
No-one that comes ever stays,
They're all just passing through.

If you take all the right turns
There's nothing left to get wrong,
Nothing is all that I have,
And now most of it's gone;
I heard of nothing before,
I know more of it now,
Learnt to play this old game
With nothing teaching me how.

I look at nothing up close,
And see there's nothing ahead;
There's nothing new I can say
That someone else hasn't said.
I know this means nothing now
But it will make sense some day,
'Cause everything in this world
Is worth nothing anyway.

Entry 16

In my life,
I never had a lot.

I started out with nothing,
And I ended up losing most of it.

But I never lost my mind.

Maybe I misplaced it a couple times

But I never lost it.

Entry 17

A few of the young guys round here have a little nickname
for me these days.

They call me *the philosopher*.

I guess 'cause sometimes, when I've had too much to
drink,

(And other times when I've not had enough to drink)

I have a tendency to start preaching shit.

Sometimes, I'll get up on a bench in town, and hold
sermon there.

Or other times I just walk around talking to myself, and
people overhear my ramblings.

Honestly, I've no idea what I say – apparently it's some
load about how the bums have all the power.

But that doesn't matter.

The point is, I've gotten this new nickname.

Which, if I'm honest, I don't mind.

It's as good a name as any.

Although, it is sort of embarrassing.

I've never once thought of myself as a philosopher.

Hell, I can barely say the word.

I suppose I always fancied myself as more of a storyteller.
'Cause to be a storyteller, all you got to be is a good liar;
And I'm a born liar.

Seriously – just think about it.
A liar makes things up for the benefit of himself.
A storyteller makes things up for the benefit of others – and that benefits himself.
(I happen to be able to do both.)

Whereas a philosopher…
A philosopher has to actually believe the things he says.
A philosopher has to be honest, intellectual, dignified, pure … he's got to be respectable.
I'm none of those things.

Entry 18

I heard it said once, that Heaven is a place on Earth.
Well, I been all over the place
And I've never found it.

I mean, you name it, I've lived there in my time.
I lived in Cities … Towns … Villages
I lived in bus stops … train stations … airports.
I lived in empty houses, under bridges, on the side of
motorways, in caravans …
Hell, I even lived in the forest for a while.

But I never found somewhere I really liked.
I never found a place I would call Heaven.
I guess 'cause every place I been, there's always a guy like
me there.

But you know what? It don't matter.
Heaven … Earth … Hell
Villages … Towns … Cities
When all said and done, every place is just the same as
everywhere else.

Living places is a lot like eating.
It don't matter what food you put in
It all ends up shit in the end.

Entry 19

The buskers in this town are so young, so clean.
But, you know what? …
To a man, every single busker I see is a hypocrite.
And it does my head in.

I remember there was this one girl I saw before.
She can't have been more than 16 years old, and she was there, with her keyboard, singing some song about heartbreak.
16 and singing about heartache!
Child, at that age you barely know where your heart is – how the hell can you know when it's breaking?

And there's this other guy I see regular.
A young guy, with dreadlocks.
He plays guitar and sings the blues.
And you know, I admit – he's got all the gear.
He's got the dreads, the voice, the facial hair, the beat up shoes … the skinny ass body.
You can't deny he's got the gear
But I swear, he's got no idea.

How do I know?

I've watched him.

I've seen him singing lyrics like *"Nobody knows me, nobody seems to care ..."*

"I ain't got nobody in this world to care for me ..."

"Here comes lonely, here comes the blues ..."

Yeah, I've seen him sing that – and then I've seen him, right after, meeting up with all his friends; all jumping on their skateboards and shit.

I've seen him of an evening too – going for drinks, or buying dinner for his girl.

I've seen him heading back home after his busking session – to his swish ass flat on the bright side of town.

He lives there with his folks and his two sisters – I've been there; I've seen them.

So he's got all that going for him – and yet he's singing that "nobody loves him – nobody cares".

What a joke.

I know some of the other guys round here are pissed off by these buskers too,

But their reasons are different than mine.

See, a lot of them see these fake ass buskers as thieves; stealing the money that should be being thrown at the feet of the tramps.

But me ... I couldn't care less about that.

The way I see it, everybody's got to try and make a penny somehow.

Some people do it by selling shit,

Others do it by buying shit,
And others do it by playing shit
(And guys like me, by sitting down and not doing shit!).

That's the way it is – and there's nothing wrong with any of it.
Like I say, everybody needs to make their pennies.

So I wouldn't say these guys are thieves and whatever.
But they still annoy the hell outta me.
Because in my mind, I see it like this:
Birds live in trees, right?
They live in nests and eat whatever the hell they can get their beaks on.

And birds sing too, don't they?

Well, when was the last time you heard a bird sing the blues?
When was the last time you heard a bird sing about heartache?

It just doesn't happen – not at all.
You know why?
Because the bird knows its own luck.
It knows it's lucky to live in a tree – because otherwise it would be living on the ground.
And it knows that it's lucky to have wings – 'cause that means it can fly, instead of having to walk everywhere.

So the way I see it, if a bird can't see no reason to sing the blues, how the hell can a 16 year old girl justify it?

How the hell can a guy with a lovely house and lovely folks and lovely friends justify it?

It's ridiculous.

He's got all that … you'd think he'd be singing a song ten times more happy than any bird.

Matter of fact, the only people who should ever be singing the blues are the ones who are lower than the birds.

People who ain't got no wings – so can't get anywhere.

People who ain't got no tree to live in, so have to sleep on the ground.

Otherwise, everything is backwards – just like it is when I watch the guy with the dreadlocks doing his thing.

'Cause there he is, singing the blues.

And here I am, living them.

Entry 20

I was standing on the corner today, just minding my own business,
And this steroid infused prick pulled up next to me.
He was cruising with the top down in some flash car
(I don't know what make it was, all I know is it was shiny as hell).
Anyway he was there, behind the wheel, wearing his two sizes too small tank top
And next to him was his pouting, orange faced girlfriend.

So the steroid guy caught me glancing, just for a second, at his flash car.
And, sniggering in his cocky ass way, he said to me
"I know you're impressed."

I looked to him slowly,
And I said
"By what?
The car?
Or the girl?"

The girl tutted, and I couldn't help but smile as she turned her face away.
Meanwhile, Mr Steroids just scoffed and said
"Both."

So, I took a moment to look a little longer at his car, then at his girl, then back to him.
Then, I shook my head
"Not my type."

Steroid guy frowned.
"What, the car? Or the girl?"

I paused for a moment, and laughed.
"Both."

Man, I can still see his face now as he drove away,
Pouting, just like his girl, and muttering cuss words.
It was one of the funniest things I seen in a long time!

Entry 21

Here's a little something I've discovered over my years.

When you're 10 years old – you want everyone to be looking at you.
When you're 20 – you hope no-one is thinking anything bad when they're looking at you.
When you're 40 – you don't care what people think when they're looking at you.
And by the time you're 60, you realise:

Nobody was looking at you.

Entry 22

The police round here, like the bar tenders, all know my name
And as such, they usually make allowances for me.

But every so often, you get some new officer on the beat;
Still learning his alphabet.
And that's really the only time I ever get problems from the guys in black and white.

Matter of fact – just last month, I had a little trouble with this new officer.

Man, this guy was a balloon.
He was strolling along the high street like some kind of school prefect – shirt all tucked in, trousers all ironed, tie fastened.
He was prim and proper …
I can't stand guys like that.
And I know for sure that guys like that can't stand me either,
So straight away, he was on my case.

He said something like "OK, come on – you can't stay there."

I didn't even look at him; just said

"What, an old man can't take a seat on the ground?"

He shot back

"No – so move along."

Now I raised my head.

I said "Man, I been moving along my entire life. So I think I'ma just stay here a little while longer. I'm not causing no trouble."

He said "Maybe not. But you are putting all these *good, honest, hardworking* people off their shopping by begging." (He made a point to really emphasise those words too: *Good, Honest, Hardworking.*)

I just laughed "Oh, really? *I'm* putting people off their shopping? Man, you're just about the first person to look at me all morning. Look around you – these people don't give a shit about me. I could be lying here dead and they wouldn't notice."

He took an impatient breath, and said "Look, I'm not arguing with you. I'm telling you. Move along. We don't allow beggars in this town."

"Well good" I said "'cause I'm not a Beggar. I'm a Bum. So you go catch those beggars and leave me alone"

He said "What's the difference?"

I was gonna tell him exactly what the difference was,
But, honestly, I couldn't be bothered to waste my time explaining anything to this clown.
So I got a little clever with him.

I said "Well, why don't *you* call *yourself* a beggar?"

He said "Because *I'm* a policeman."

I said "Well, *I'm* a Bum. Same difference."

He scoffed "Bums, beggars – whatever, you're all the same."

Well, that really got me fired up.

I looked him dead in the eye, and said

"Look here, child. Have I begged you for anything?

Have I approached any person this morning? Even once?

No. No. No.

My whole life, I never begged for nothing.

I never even begged somebody's pardon.

Not like you.

I bet you had to do a whole lot of begging before they gave you that dumb ass uniform."

I smiled when I finished talking, because I could see he didn't like being called "Child". His face went all red and his eyes darkened.

I thought *"Damn right, too … don't nobody call me a beggar."*

He said "Look, I've been polite. But now I'm serious. Move along."

I didn't move a muscle – just stared at him.

He said "If you're going to act like an infant, I can count to three if you like."

I said "You can count to whatever the hell number you like. I'm not moving."

Well, with that, he lost his cool. He grabbed me by the arm, and dragged me to my feet.

I put up a little fight – but not much. My old bones don't

let me fight like I used to, so I just wriggled and flayed a bit until he pinned me against the wall and handcuffed me.

Credit where credit's due; this guy might have been a balloon – but he was a strong balloon.

The rest of that day is a bit of a blur. But I was taken down to the police station, and ended up spending two nights there. It was horrific.

A guy like me ain't built to live under roofs, or in the middle of walls.

So the whole time, I was anxious as hell.

It felt like I'd been buried alive.

I didn't have no drink.

No cigarettes.

And worst of all, the clown took my book away.

So for two days and two nights, I had nothing to write and nothing to read.

I was scared he had burnt it or something, as an extra punishment.

But luckily, when they came to kick me out, it was an officer I knew and she gave me it back with no damage.

She also said she had had a word with the son of a bitch who put me in there, and he agreed that, from now on, he'd look the other way when he saw me – but only if, first, I apologised to him for being so obnoxious.

Well, I didn't apologise.

But she told him I had.

And since then, he hasn't given me any hassle.

So I can't be too mad at the guy.

Although it woulda been a different story if he had gone and done anything to my book.

I don't know what I'd do without it – I sure as hell can't afford a new one.

And even if I could, I don't think I could remember half the shit I've written in here.

Entry 23

I've not been able to afford a drink for a couple days.
I had a few swigs from a couple of empty cans I found today (I chose to believe it was beer and not piss I was drinking).
But nothing else.

It's fucking hard, man.
Seriously.
See, when I'm not drinking ... I get to thinking.
And for a guy like me, thinking is never good.

I mean, drinking is no good either.
But it's much better than thinking.

See, I have this little saying
Which goes like this:

Drinking fills a man until he's dead,
But thinking kills a man while he's alive.

And that's the truth.

Entry 24

Man, my problem has always been the same;
I see too much.
I have this nasty habit of looking places at the wrong time,
And seeing things I should never have seen.

Every single day of my life, I see some other shit that would
break my heart (if it hadn't already been broken, shattered,
and stamped into the ground) –
And there aint a thing I can do about any of it.
Not a damn thing.
I drink till my vision blurs, and I still see it all.
I go to sleep, and I dream it all again.

I see guys acting up,
Girls acting up,
Husbands mistreating their wives,
Mother's mistreating their children,
Children shouting shit at old people,
Cussing and swearing.

I see guys wasting their life
And girls selling themselves too cheap.

I see dealers handing children their first hit,
And then I watch as those same children come back again and again
Before eventually they become the dealers themselves.

Honestly, it's fucking pandemonium out here.
And the world calls me a drunk?

Well, from what I see, I'm not drunk.
I'm sober.
It's the rest of the world that's drunk.

Entry 25

I could've married once or twice.
I think I'd liked to have taken a wife.

When I was a kid, I knew this girl called Francesca –
Chesca, for short.

Chesca was a good four or five years younger than I was;
she was still in school when I had long since been kicked
out.
But she lived round my estate, so I used to see her around
all the time.
She was always out and about, getting up to something or
another – either with her group of little school friends, or
with one of her little sisters (her mother was the kind of
woman who saw having kids as a profession – at the time,
she had four girls and a little baby boy, all by different
men).

Well, back then, I still used to spend a lot of time on my
own – just hanging around my estate, making the place
look untidy.
Of an evening, I might go and hang with a few guys down

in the town – my friends at the time were all fifty/sixty year old gambling addicts and alcoholics.

But mostly, as I say, I would be on my own – not too different from these days.

But, as she got a little older, Chesca got a little bolder.

She started coming up and talking with me – asking me to buy her cigarettes and such. (I always agreed.)

And pretty soon, she ditched her friends and started hanging out with me regular.

Who knows why … but she did.

I mean, I sure as hell didn't encourage her;

But then, I didn't discourage her either.

I guess it was an ego trip – to have a girl following me around, trying to impress me.

It made me feel big.

And even though Chesca hadn't exactly grown into the best looking girl – she was alright.

Better than nothing.

But I remember after a while, her mother started getting more and more on my case.

She told me that Chesca had been skipping school (which I already knew) and she called me a bad influence.

And you know, looking back now, I agree with her.

A bad influence is the only kind of influence I was ever good at being.

But back then, I didn't give a shit what her mother thought.

In fact, I didn't really give a shit about Chesca either.

I could have taken her or left her – it was all the same to me.

It was only that, at that time, getting my kicks for free from Chesca was easier than having to pay some other girly for them; which is what all the other guys I knew used to do.

Chesca was convenient for me – that's exactly how I saw it.

I was having my fun, and as far as I was concerned, that was all that mattered.

Man, I was one selfish son of a bitch.

And poor Chesca – she didn't even see what an asshole I really was.

She honestly thought I was the real thing … that she was in love with me.

And maybe she was – I don't know.

Now I'm old, I sometimes think maybe … maybe I could have loved her too – eventually.

I don't know.

I just know that, if I could go back now … I would try to love her.

I really would.

Anyway, pretty soon, all that became irrelevant.

Because two weeks after Chesca's seventeenth birthday, she told me she was pregnant.

My first thought was "*Shit – you've really fucking screwed up this time*" followed by "*How the hell am I gonna get outta this?*"

See, as always, just thinking about myself.

It never even entered my thick ass head to think of how this must have been for Chesca.

I mean, she was just a kid,

And there she was, saying she was gonna *have* a kid.

My kid.

Well, something like a week after she told me, Chesca came clean to her mother as well.

And man, she went ballistic.

I remember this day, I was hanging around on the estate green (which was just over the road from Chesca's place) when I saw her mother come tearing outta their house.

Straight away, she spotted me – and came hurtling over.

Almost before I could react, this woman was on me.

She damn knocked me off my feet, and started beating me to hell – all the time, screaming "You fucking asshole!" over and over.

And you know... I wish I could say that I took it like a man.

I wish I could say that I didn't fight back, because of respect for women and such – but that would be a lie.

Truth is, I wanted to fight back –

Hell, I tried to fight back;

I just couldn't.

This woman was too much for me.

She was crazy.

And I bet she would have gone all the way and beat me straight to death, if Chesca hadn't stepped in and dragged her off 'a me.

'Cause even after she had stopped laying into me, she was full of threats.

Her last words to me were

"You Asshole! You're dead, you know that. I know people. And you're fucking dead!"

I believed every word too.

Like I said, this woman was crazy.

So Chesca went and escorted her rabid mother back into their house, and, from what she told me afterwards, the two of them had the biggest fight.

Apparently, it even got physical at one point – and ended with Chesca storming outta the house, with her mother shouting after her "That's it. Piss off. Go stay with that scumbag, 'cause you're not welcome here anymore. You stupid little girl."

Now, I was still basically where I had been earlier – nursing my wounds (I'm pretty sure the bitch broke my nose that day … I never been able to breathe outta it since).

So Chesca came back over, and apologised for what had happened.

She had a few scratches on her face, but she wasn't crying or nothing – to be honest, she was still pretty pumped up, and was just going on about how her mother was a bitch and such.

Then, she started going on about how she was sick of it all round here; that she wanted to get outta this place.

More specifically, she wanted us to run away together.

I remember, she'd been mentioning shit like this for months beforehand – saying how her and me should run away together, and be like Bonnie and Clyde.

I used to just grin and brush it off, figuring to myself *"Just let her have her fantasies – that's all they are."*

Only this time, she was serious.

This wasn't a daydream like before – this was a stone cold suggestion.

She said it would be beautiful – we could go someplace away from parents or friends or neighbours … some place where it would be just the two of us.

We could both get jobs, rent a little place and raise this kid right.

Bear in mind, as she was saying all this, I was still pretty damn groggy from the beating I had just gotten from her mother.

And after a beating like that, I admit I was feeling pretty pissed off with the place too.

So when she finished, and said "What do you think?" –

Well, I didn't think.

I just spoke.

I said "Yeah, you know what – let's do it. Fuck this place … we could go live somewhere ten times better than this shithole."

I knew as soon as I heard it coming outta my mouth that it was all bullshit.

I was just being temperamental … 'cause really, there was no way I wanted to leave.

That estate … that area … it was a dump –

But it was *my* dump.

And if things had been different, I'd have probably stayed there for my whole life – maybe turned into one of those sixty year old gamblers I used to know.

But no – I said what I said.
I'd agreed with her.
She had gotten all excited,
And now, I couldn't take it back.
I was stuck – and it was no joke.
First thing in the morning, me and Chesca were gonna be on the first train out of there.

It started getting late, so we left the green and I walked Chesca round to one of her old school friend's place, where she was gonna spend that night.
(She had wanted to spend the night with me, but I said she couldn't. Mostly because I didn't want her to – but also because, at that time, I used to sleep on the couch in a bedsit flat which belonged to two of my friends from the bars – so, even if I'd wanted her to stay with me, there would have been no space.)
So I left her there at her friend's place, with the promise that, first thing the next morning, I'd meet her down at the train station.

When I think back now, the only person I feel sorry for is Chesca.
She was the victim in all of this.
But that night, when the bars had all closed and I was walking up and down the town on my own, the only person I felt sorry for was myself.

I just kept thinking *"This is too heavy. This is way too heavy.*

I'm twenty two years old … I should be free to do whatever the fuck I like.

Now all of a sudden I'm running away with some girl I don't even really like?

And we're gonna be raising some kid I don't even want?

No.

We were just fooling around. If any more came of it, it's her fault … not mine.

This thing … it's her kid … she's the one who wants it – not me.

It's nothing to do with me.

If she wants to raise it, let her. But I sure as hell ain't gonna be no baby's Daddy."

Well, I never went back to the bedsit that night.

And, when that night was over – and the day came – I never showed up at the station either.

Just like the selfish, good for nothing bum that I am, I stood Chesca up.

No word, no explanation, no apology – nothing.

And you know, it kills me to think of her – sitting on the platform, all alone.

Or standing outside the station, looking this way and that. She probably had the tickets in her hand, hope in her heart, and a bag full of belongings on her back.

To this day, it still kills me.

Three days later, I came outta hiding.

64

And the first thing I did was catch sight of the local paper
outside a shop in town.
On the front page was a picture.
It was of Chesca.
And the headline:
Teenage Girl
Throws herself in front of train.
Dead.

I left town that very second, and I never been back since.

Entry 26

My last entry, I spoke about Chesca.

So, while I'm at it, I'ma just continue along those lines again

And talk about Grace.

The girl who was the closest thing to a soul mate I ever had.

Grace was a hooker from up North.

She'd been in the game for around about ten years when I met her, but man

She wasn't like all those other ones.

She had Elegance,

Radiance,

Class …

She was an angel in a sinner's world.

Anyway, I first met Grace at a time when I'd just started living in a tent on the corner of a little place the locals used to call "The Dirty Mile".

Now, most every town has a Dirty Mile (and, in my experience, if a town hasn't got a dirty mile, then the whole place is dirty!).

See, The Dirty Mile is the dark place – on the outskirts of town – where all the misfits and the down and outs gather. It's that area where any normal person would want to stay well clear of – especially when the sun goes down.

And that's exactly where I was living.

So by day, The Dirty Mile was full of beggars, addicts and drug dealers.

And by night, when all the amber lights came on,

The dealers would head into town,

The beggars would find a little spot to lay down for the night,

And a whole new crowd patrolled The Dirty Mile – mostly, pimps and prostitutes.

As it happens, these days, almost nobody works The Dirty Mile anymore.

It's all just tramps and bums here now – kinda like a little gypsy camp for anyone who's going nowhere.

But back then, rain or shine there would be at least fifteen, if not twenty, girlys on any given night.

And Grace was one of them.

To this day, I can still see her ... strolling up and down the Mile ... talking to passers-by, or gathered with some of the other girls.

She had this way of walking, that was like ... it seemed like she was standing still, and the whole street was moving underneath her.

I've never seen anything like it.

And I just remember, every night I used to watch her get into some blacked out car, or go off with some guy … and I swear, I would pray for her.

Man, I had no fucking idea who the hell I was praying to – but I would genuinely be on my knees, praying that she would get back safe.

Praying that I would see her again.

Not that I was gonna do anything if I did see her again.

I never had the guts to go up and speak to her.

But just *seeing* her … just knowing she was still alive … that was all I ever wanted.

Well, she always did come back safe.

And as time went on, to my surprise, she even started acknowledging me.

First she'd flash me one of her little lonely smiles here and there.

Then one day, she said hello – and asked for a sip of my drink.

And before I knew it, me and Grace would talk every day.

I always remember how she used ask me a lot questions; she was always curious about me and my experiences.

And I'd tell her anything she wanted; from whatever shit I'd seen that day, right through to all the other shit I'd been through on the streets.

You know; most every person I've ever known – and this includes myself – has always seen me as nothing but a bum and a good for nothing.

That's it.

But Grace … she listened to my stories, and she saw me for something else.

I remember she once said to me "I don't think you're a good for nothing … not at all. I think you're just like me. You're too sensitive, and that's why you turn to things like drink – to escape from a world which is just too much too bear."

Man, she was right.

I knew it then, and I know it now – she was right.

She knew me better than I knew myself.

Pretty soon, I started asking her more about her own life too.

And boy, she'd been to even more places than I had.

She told me how she was a City girl, born and raised

How she'd lived in Paris for a while, then Rome, and then Amsterdam,

She told me how she'd fallen into the game in her early twenties, when she moved back to this country, and how she'd been jumping from place to place ever since.

And with any story she ever told me about her life as a hooker, she always ended it with saying the same thing;

She always finished by saying how she was trying to get outta of it all.

Well, one night, when we had been talking for the best part of two hours, I asked why she couldn't get out. What was stopping her?

I remember she smiled the saddest little smile I ever saw, and said

"Cause right now, I've got not no place else to go.
And I don't want to be alone."

This straight up hit me like a freight train.

I'd been thinking the exact same thing to myself for years:
"How can you move on, when you've got no place to go?"
And I'd never found the answer.

But a statement like that, coming from an angel like Grace
... it seemed somehow different than when it was coming
from a bum like me.
For me, there was no hope.
But for her – there was.
She *could* move on – she could become whatever she
wanted.
She didn't have to end up alone like I had.

So I said to her "But Grace, don't you see? You ain't got to
know where you're going – you just have to know where
you want to get away from.
If you want to find something new, you ain't got to know
where you're gonna find it.
You don't even have to know what it is you're looking for.
All you gotta do is start searching.
As long as you're searching for something ... you can find
anything.
And it don't matter what it is.
You don't need a house to make a home.
Home can be a tent on a street corner, or the end of a park
bench. As long as *you're* there, it's home..."

I paused a moment.

I thought I had said all that I had to say.

But pretty soon, a whole bunch of other words started pouring out too.

"See, the way I see it … for people like you and me, there ain't gonna be no fairytale.

There ain't gonna be no pots of gold … but it doesn't mean we can't still chase rainbows.

I mean, look at me.

My whole life, I never had no place to be – but I always end up somewhere.

And one of these days, you … me … all the lonely people; we'll all find our place.

Trust me, it's out there. It's out there right now.

And who knows, maybe it will be the same place.

Just imagine that. You and me … we could go anywhere.

And all the time we were together, we'd have a friend in every place in the world.

You could follow me, and I could follow you … We'd never be lonely again.

Maybe we'd find us a forest somewhere; live off the land. Get away from all the people that never needed us. Away from all the cities … all the towns … all the Dirty Miles. Anything's possible.

But we just got to start heading there, right now.

Even if we don't know where 'there' is yet – we can still head there. You understand?"

With that, I stopped.

I knew I'd said too much.

Straight away, I knew I'd said far too much.

We sat in silence for the longest time,
And then finally she whispered
"If … If I quit …
Will you help me?
I mean, will you promise that you'll *always* help me … that you'll never leave me?"

I looked back at her, and said
"Grace – if you asked me to, I'd give you this tent of mine, put on your high heel boots and go take your place out there on the Mile."

She laughed, and I could see her eyes glisten with tears.
Then she turned her gaze straight ahead, and I did the same.

We sat on the corner together – just like that – for the entire night.
We watched cars coming and going – girls going, and coming back again.
People walking up and down, and all around The Dirty Mile.
And Grace never moved.
She just sat right there, next to me, and we watched the sun come up together.
And for the first time in twenty good for nothing years of my good for nothing life,
I smiled.

Well, after that night, Grace did get out of the game.
And for a while, she came to live with me – in my tent on
the corner.
It was – and is still – the single period of happiness I ever
had.
We were two bums, living in a one man tent,
Sleeping side by side, and sharing everything.
Grace was my wife, my girlfriend, my sister, my daughter,
my best friend. She was my everything.
And it was beautiful because it wasn't us against the world –
It was us in our *own* world.
Nothing else mattered.
Only Grace.

I remember I even went and got myself a little day job, so
I could buy her a few luxuries (nothing fancy – maybe a
packet of cigarettes, or a cup of coffee here and there).
It was around Christmas time, and I used to go collecting
shit to recycle … so, filling up these big ass sacks full of
cans and bottles and such – then going on over to sell it at
the local tip.
It's funny, I remember catching sight of myself in a shop
window at one point, and thinking "*Man, I look like Santa
Clause's down and out half-brother!*"

But I kept up my working straight into the New Year, and
things were going pretty well.

Then one evening, in the last week of February, I came
back to the tent after a day down town,
And Grace wasn't there.

Just over the road, there were already a few girlys who had started work for the evening – all standing in a little group talking.

So I went over to speak to them, to ask if they'd seen Grace,

And they told me that they had.

They said that, about a half hour ago, they had seen her getting into some car and being driven off.

Now these girls could be real malicious bitches sometimes, so I hoped that they were lying –

But, deep down, I knew they weren't.

So, I trudged back over to my corner; furious and terrified.

Furious because I knew this meant Grace was with a client – and she swore to me she was done with all that shit.

But mostly terrified, because I know the way the world works.

"The last go" is always the one where something goes wrong.

"One more won't hurt" is always when you get hurt.

And I knew that this time, Grace wouldn't be coming back.

I could feel it.

Something bad had happened.

Or was about to happen.

But I was wrong.

Late that night, she did come back.

And I should have been happy.

I should have smiled, and said hello;

And been grateful.

But instead, as soon as I saw her,

I straight up launched into an interrogation.

I asked her where she'd been – and she flat out lied to my face.

She said she had been down in the town, having a coffee catch up with one of the other girlys of The Dirty Mile.

I told her she was talking bullshit.

I said I knew she had sold herself – that she had broken her promise.

I said "And I bet it's not the only time either is it?"

And with that, she started crying.

I didn't even try to comfort her or nothing – I just watched as the tears rolled down her perfect cheeks.

Eventually, she came clean.

Yes, she had been with a customer.

An old guy, who she used to see before.

And no, it wasn't the only time … she had been seeing him for the past three weeks.

But, she claimed that she'd only done it because she wanted to help out … that she felt bad about me having to work for her, and so she figured, if she made a little money herself …

I never listened to the rest of her explanation.

I just held my hand up and said

"Enough of this shit. I don't want to hear another word. I'm done."

I made to walk away, and Grace, in tears again, tried to grab me.

She took a hold of my arm, but I just pushed her away, calling her a whore.

She fell to the floor.

And, looking down at her one more time, I said the coldest words to ever come outta my mouth.
I said "I never want to see you again."

Then I spat on the tent (she could keep it, I didn't care) – and I walked away.

Well, I can't remember what I did after that.
I can't remember where I spent that night,
And I can't remember where I woke up.
But I know that the next day, I was a wreck.
I straight up hated myself for everything I had said –
I'd been such a fucking asshole.

So what if Grace lied when she promised she was out of the game for good?
She wasn't lying just for the fun of it.
Shit, she was sacrificing herself for our sake – for *my* sake.
And what had I done?
I'd been an ungrateful, small minded, temperamental prick.

So, that morning, I returned to The Dirty Mile,
I returned to the corner, as quick as I could.
And the tent was still there –
But Grace wasn't.

Turns out that, just after I stormed off the previous night, she had disappeared.
Without a word or a line.
And this time, no-one saw where she'd gone.

I desperately asked around, hoping that I'd find just one person who knew where she'd gone;
Even just one person who may have seen the direction she had gone in.
Seriously, I was pushing and pleading –
I was hassling strangers –
I was questioning everyone I saw like a fucking madman.

But no-one knew a thing.
Not a damn thing.

So, with nothing else to try, I sat down on the corner, next to the tent.
In the same spot where we had sat together.
And I waited.

I waited for a week, without moving an inch.
But no Grace.
I waited for a year, for two years, for ten years.
But no Grace.
And to this day, I have waited near on twenty-nine years for her.

And you know what ... I will carry on waiting too.
I'll wait for her until the day I die.
Hell, I'll even wait here after I die too if I can.

But I know it's all over.
I know I'll never see Grace again.
I'll never even get to know what happened to her.

So, there you have it.
I left Chesca at the station,
And Grace left me at the corner.

I guess that evens up the score.

Entry 27

You know, something else I learnt over the years is this:
Everybody's running from something.
Don't matter who they are or what they do – everybody's got a secret they can't face.
Everybody's got a regret they can't shake.
Everybody's got some kind of demon following them.

I met a guy once, who used to be known as "The Runner".
He was a guy you'd see every single day round here – without fail.
And he was always running.
Wasn't a young guy either – I had him down for a solid sixty.
But he was always running … up and down, through the town, all over the place.
He was hard to miss 'cause he'd always be bare footed (he used to say his feet got claustrophobic) and shirtless – no matter the weather.

I remember hearing once that he used to cover thirty miles a day – sometimes more.
And I wouldn't bet against it. The guy was dedicated as hell.

But for years, I used to watch him run past me on the corner – once in the morning, and then back again later in the evening.

And I used to just wonder *"what's he running from?"*

'Cause nobody runs that far if they're trying to get somewhere.

The way I see it, if you're going somewhere, then, when you get there, you stop.

You're there … you've made it … and that's the end of it.

The only people who keep on going are the ones who are still trying to get away from something.

So I'd look at him running, and think "Ma*n, something heavy must be on his trail."*

Well, some nights, The Runner used to come hang out on The Dirty Mile with the rest of us good for nothings.

I never heard him say much.

And never heard anybody say much to him.

Looking back, I don't even know why he used to hang out there to be honest.

I never got the impression that he was there to get girls or drugs or anything like that.

And he always just looked pretty out of place amongst the rest of us – as if he was a sober violinist in a drunk man's orchestra.

But I guess he was just there because he had no place else to be.

Anyway, one night, I happened to get to talking with him.

It was the one and only time, but man, the things he told me – I'll never forget it.

See, it turned out that he used to be this top city lawyer.

And when I say top, I mean seriously the *top* –

I'm talking six/seven figures a year salary,

Flash motor,

House in the city,

Place abroad…

This guy was the real deal.

Well, after 25 years working and flying high, he got given this murder case.

He didn't tell me all the details, but even the basics were fucking horrific.

He was on prosecution.

The poor victims were a grandmother and her little grand-daughter,

But the killers were just kids – two fourteen year olds and one twelve year old.

Apparently they'd gone in to rob the place, and come out as murderers.

Just awful, tragic, horrific, messed up shit.

He told me that, right from the off, this case had been affecting him in ways it shouldn't have.

He'd been through murder trials before – tons of them – but this was different.

This was messing with his head.

And though he tried to get on with it, midway through the case, my man The Runner couldn't take any more.

He told me how, this one day, the court took a mid-morning break, and he stepped outside to get some air.
He said to me "I was standing outside the courtroom, and the whole fucking world started caving in on me. My head had just gone … all I could do was fall to my knees and sob
"And in that moment … I didn't know who I was, where I was or why I was there … I just knew I had to get out.
"So I got up from the floor, still sobbing, and I started walking. But honestly, the buildings were bearing down on me. They were reaching out to grab me. And all the people were staring … leering.
"I started walking faster – then jogging – then sprinting. And all the time, I was whipping off another bit of clothing, until I was running in nothing but my pants.
"I didn't know where I was going … but I knew what I had to get away from. And that was *everything*. I couldn't stay in the city for another second. And I couldn't go home either – this stuff knew where I lived…
"So, I just kept on going and going and going."

He finished talking, and I remember just shaking my head in disbelief.
I said to him "Man, so you been running ever since?"
He shrugged, and said
"Like they say, everybody's running from something."

Entry 28

Not all tramps or bums are good for nothing's like me.
A lot of them are the most intelligent, sensitive, conscious
people you could ever meet.

They're in tune with the world more than any other type
of person.
Why?
Because they're living in it.
They're not living in a palace, or a house, or an apartment.
They're not living for a job, or a car, or a girl.
That's the kind of shit that makes you deluded.
No, tramps and bums are living in the world – every single
day.
They're coming straight from reality.
And that's the truth.

So you can forget about all these kings and queens and
politicians and presidents.
To a man, they are all full of air.
You want to know about the world?
Talk to the tramps and the bums.
That's where the wisdom is.

Entry 29

It's crazy to overhear people talking sometimes.
And to get a sense of the things they think are important.
People say *"It's important I do this.*
It's important I get that.
It's important that I make this bus – otherwise …"

Otherwise what?
You'll get the next bus, that's all.

Then they say something like
"But I'll have wasted a bunch of time"

Child, you say that like it's a bad thing.

Everything we do is just to waste a bunch of time.
What difference does it make whether you waste your
time waiting for a bus, or writing a poem?
At the end of the day, it's all just a distraction.

We're all just killing time until time eventually kills us.

Entry 30

You know, I've lived all this time.
And I've never once been good at anything.
That's bad, right.
Never been good at a single thing.
And not only that, but never even tried to be good at anything.

I spent the first half of my life waiting around to live.
And I've spent this last half just waiting around to die.

Entry 31

Sometimes I wonder – why in hell was someone like me given the chance to be in this world?
I'm serious.
This ain't no teenage, existential angst.
This aint no mid-life crisis.

See, I picture the time before life – the time before birth – as like a job interview.
So you've got The Boss,
And He's got a position going in his building.
And there are all these people who've applied; who are desperate to get the job.

So The Boss spends a little time going through their application forms.
He conducts a few interviews.
And then chooses who to hire.

Whoever gets the job, gets born.
And whoever doesn't, has to wait for another position to come up.

But if that's the case, then I can't help but think,

How the fuck did I get this job?
And why?
I mean, there must have been so many other candidates –
far better than me.
Guys who would have worked hard
Tried hard
Contributed a lot.
Guys who would have been good team members
And who could have gone on to achieve anything they liked.

But instead, they hired me.
Me.
A guy who was born a good for nothing
Grew up a waste of space
And ended up a drunk and a bum.
It makes no sense.
I mean, even *I* wouldn't have hired me.

The only thing I can think of is this:
Maybe my application got mixed up with someone else's.
Maybe I got given this job 'cause they thought I was
somebody else.

Man, I feel so bad for that other guy.
I really do.

I just hope he managed to score some other position in
this business.
'Cause if he didn't – he must be looking at me, and be
fucking furious.

Entry 32

I write the words
That no-one reads
I give advice
Nobody heeds
Not even me.

I ain't got a job
Don't have a home
I travel light
On roads of stone
And all alone.

I made my bed
And that's where I lay
Don't look at me
Don't look away
What can I say?

Been here a while
Soon I'll be gone
I don't need anyone
To tell me I'm wrong

I knew it all along

I knew it all along

I knew it all along

Entry 33

Man, the people of this world never cared for me.
They never needed me.

But, as much as I have tried to put on a face
To ignore them.
As much as I have tried to say I never cared for them, and
I don't need anyone.
I've lied.

If I could start again, someplace else.

I would take all the time I spent learning how to be alone.
And use it as time to spend learning how to not be alone.

Entry 34

To every place I've ever been; sorry for making a mess.

To every person who ever gave me a penny; thank you.

To every person who ever saw me at my best; remember me.

To every person who ever saw me at my worst; forgive me.

If you're a bum; I hope you read these words and never try to be anything else.

And if you're not a bum; I hope you read these words and make sure you never become one.

Chesca; I'm sorry.

Grace; I hope you're happy, wherever you are.

I'm out of pages.

I'm out of drink.

I'm out of time.

I want to go home.

This heart-breaking passage was the final entry in the diary. Written, as The Old Drunk says, on the very last page.

It was, in all likelihood, the very last thing he ever wrote; and I would imagine that he died soon after writing it – although, of course, I will never know for sure how, when or where he met his end.

Throughout the diary, there are many entries which are fairly depressing in tone, and which seem to be The Old Drunk trying to make some kind of peace with his inevitable, and increasingly near, end. But this particular entry seems to go deeper than those before it. To me, it seems to suggest that, when he wrote those final words "I want to go home", The Old Drunk knew that these really were to be his final words ...

But, though this last entry was the conclusion to the writings of The Old Drunk – there is one more chapter to this story.

Because, on the inside of the back cover of the book, there was one more, rather surprising, entry.

It was written in a completely different hand to the rest of the book – a far smaller and more precise hand.

Again, there is unfortunately no way of discovering who wrote it or when it was written. In fact, the writer of this additional entry is, if anything, even more mysterious, and elusive, than The Old Drunk himself.

By what is written, we can know fairly confidently that it was written by a man – and we can reasonably assume that the writer also lives/works on the streets. But that is all.
(If I had to guess, I would say that it was written by someone who at the very least knew of The Old Drunk while he was still alive – and, being something of a romantic, I like to go even further, and believe that they may well have even known him personally.)

I have decided to add it on here for two reasons.

Firstly, because, when I came across it for the first time, I found it to be a strangely comforting thing to read after all that had passed before it. It was proof to me that I was not the only person to have ever been touched by these words. And though I had no clue who this person was, it was almost like meeting a kindred spirit.

But secondly – perhaps more importantly – I have included it because, in my eyes, it is the the perfect way to bring the diary to a close.
Where we started with The Old Drunk saying why he was writing these words, we finish with a reader of those words saying how he feels now, having read them.
It is a poignant and extremely deserving tribute to this remarkable man.

And as such, I have decided to title it A Eulogy to the Old Drunk.

Entry 35

My friend.

You were right.

Guys like you … guys like me …people like us – we don't get funerals.

We don't get gravestones or obituaries.

We don't get horse drawn carriages.

When we're gone; we're *Real Gone*.

But you … you're not like the rest of us.

Your words will remain, and your memory will live on.

You may have gone. But you will *never* be Real Gone.

And you know something?

Maybe the people never needed you.

Maybe the world never wanted you.

But we are, all of us, far worse off without you.

You were the deepest, the craziest, the maddest and the baddest of us all.

So on behalf of everyone working the streets – in this town, and the next.

On behalf of all us bums, tramps, hobos, hustlers, pimps, prostitutes, dealers, dossers, down and outs and good for

nothings – I want to say thank you.
Thank you for your words,
Thank you for your thoughts,
Thank you for choosing our streets to live on.

I hope you find your little corner somewhere out there in
the stars.

I hope you're watching from some place, as the next Bum
reads your diary.

And, if you didn't make it to Heaven,
I know for sure that the devil had a drink waiting for you
in Hell.

I imagine that would be more your style anyway.